BAGDASARIAN
PRODUCTIONS

ALVINNN!!!
AND THE CHIPMUNKS™
The Best Video Game Ever

adapted by Lauren Forte
based on the screenplay "Mystic Mountain"
written by Reid Harrison

Ready-to-Read

Simon Spotlight

New York   London   Toronto   Sydney   New Delhi

SIMON SPOTLIGHT
An imprint of Simon & Schuster Children's Publishing Division
1230 Avenue of the Americas, New York, New York 10020
This Simon Spotlight edition August 2017
For information about special discounts for bulk purchases, please contact
Simon & Schuster Special Sales at 1-866-506-1949 or business@simonandschuster.com.
Manufactured in the United States of America 0717 LAK
10 9 8 7 6 5 4 3 2 1
ISBN 978-1-5344-0048-1 (hc)
ISBN 978-1-5344-0047-4 (pbk)
ISBN 978-1-5344-0049-8 (eBook)

"Hey, fellas?" Dave called out when he arrived home. *This house is way too quiet,* he thought. He wondered where everyone was.

"Boys?" Dave said, peeking
into their room.
"Close the door!" Theodore yelled.
"We can't see our screens in
the light."
"What are you doing?" Dave asked.

"We're playing Mystic Mountain Adventure," Alvin answered.
"Can we talk later, Dave?" Simon begged.
"Fine," Dave agreed with a groan.

Dave worked all day
trying to write a new song,
but he was not getting very far.
He decided to check on everyone
again.

"The light!" Theodore cried out
as Dave opened the door.
"You're still playing?"
Dave asked, surprised.
He told them they needed to
take a break from screen time.

"Why?!" the boys yelled together.
"You've never even played
the game," said Simon.
"Maybe you should give it a chance!"
Dave agreed to try it out.

"First thing you do is create
your username," Simon explained.
"Make it something fun."
Dave typed as Theodore
and Simon watched.

Ding! Ding! the computer sounded.
"Hey, what happened?" Dave asked.
"That was Alvin stealing some of
your gear," said Simon.

"Alvin! You can't steal from me!"
Dave shouted into his headset.
"Actually, I can," Alvin said
from his room. "It's part of the game."
Ding! Ding!

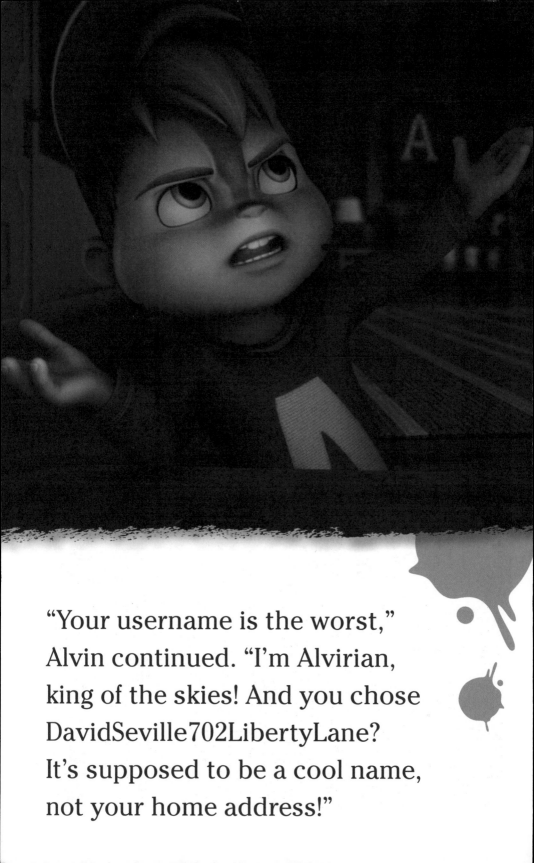

"Your username is the worst," Alvin continued. "I'm Alvirian, king of the skies! And you chose DavidSeville702LibertyLane? It's supposed to be a cool name, not your home address!"

"Geez, why don't you just give
out *all* your personal
information," Theo complained.
The boys went back upstairs
and left Dave to figure
it out on his own.

The next morning, when the
Chipmunks came in for breakfast,
they were in for a shock.
"Look at this mess!"
Theodore complained.

When they went to Dave's room,
they got an even bigger surprise.
He'd been playing all night,
and his desk was covered
with garbage and crumbs!

"Dave, what has happened to you?"
asked Simon.

"Guys—can't talk," Dave said quickly.
"My castle is under attack by
Lorgard the goblin king!"

So the boys went to school.
"What are we going to do
about Dave?" Simon asked.
As they rounded the hallway,
they saw Kevin and his friends.

"Your father stole my sword of a thousand visions," he said angrily. "How do you know it was our dad?" asked Theodore.

"Who else would
DavidSeville702LibertyLane be?"
Kevin answered.
"He took *all* our gear,"
argued someone else.
"You had better control your dad!"
Kevin declared before leaving.

When the boys got home
that afternoon, Dave was in even
worse shape.
"Light!" Dave screamed.

"Dave, we feel you should
stop playing Mystic Mountain,"
Simon said.
"What? Why?" Dave asked, not even
looking up from the monitor.

"You're looting from everyone,"
Simon answered.

"Real people with real feelings."

"So? Alvin loots!" Dave cried.

"Only from you," Alvin replied.

"Not from other players!"

But before anyone could
say another word,
Dave grabbed his computer,
bolted away, and
locked himself in the bathroom.

Just then the phone rang,
and Theodore answered it.
"Guys! That was Kevin!
Dave is still looting.
There's going to be a war on our
castle . . .
I mean, our house!"

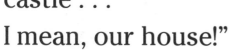

"Hear that, Dave?" Alvin called
through the door.
"We have to protect our castle!"
"Like Mystic Mountain?"
asked Theodore.
"Only real!" Simon replied.

The Chipettes joined in to help.
Battle plans were drawn.

Supplies were prepared.

And the castle was protected
by the fighters, ready for battle.

When Kevin and his army
arrived, he yelled,
"Surrender the computer!"
"Not gonna happen," Alvin hollered
back.
"Then it's war!" Kevin shouted.
"Charge!"

Kevin and his team let out a roar as they came through the gate.

Trip wires were pulled.

Water buckets were emptied.

And water balloons and tomatoes were thrown.

Then the phone rang with a reminder
for Dave that he had a song to finish.
"Oh no! I completely forgot,"
he moaned from behind the door.
"Give up the game," Simon begged.
"We can still fix things!"

Dave finally gave up and came out for a sit-down with Kevin. "Thank you for calling a truce," Kevin said. "But I've come for your game."

Dave handed over the game disk. "I'm embarrassed about the way I behaved," he said sheepishly to the boys. "I think that's a lesson for all of us," Simon agreed.

The boys and the Chipettes
helped Dave finish his song.
As they sang into the phone,
David said, "I have the best secret
weapons!"
The Chipmunks and the Chipettes
saved the day!